This Little Tiger book belongs to:

_____

_____

_____

_____

For Marion x ~ A R

For Nicole and David x x x ~ H G

LITTLE TIGER PRESS
1 The Coda Centre,
189 Munster Road, London SW6 6AW
www.littletigerpress.com

First published in Great Britain 2012
This edition published 2013
Text copyright © Alison Ritchie 2012
Illustrations copyright © Hannah George 2012
Alison Ritchie and Hannah George have asserted their rights
to be identified as the author and illustrator of this work
under the Copyright, Designs and Patents Act, 1988
A CIP catalogue record for this book
is available from the British Library

ISBN 978-1-84895-316-1
LTP/1400/0521/1112
Printed in China
10 9 8 7 6 5 4 3 2 1

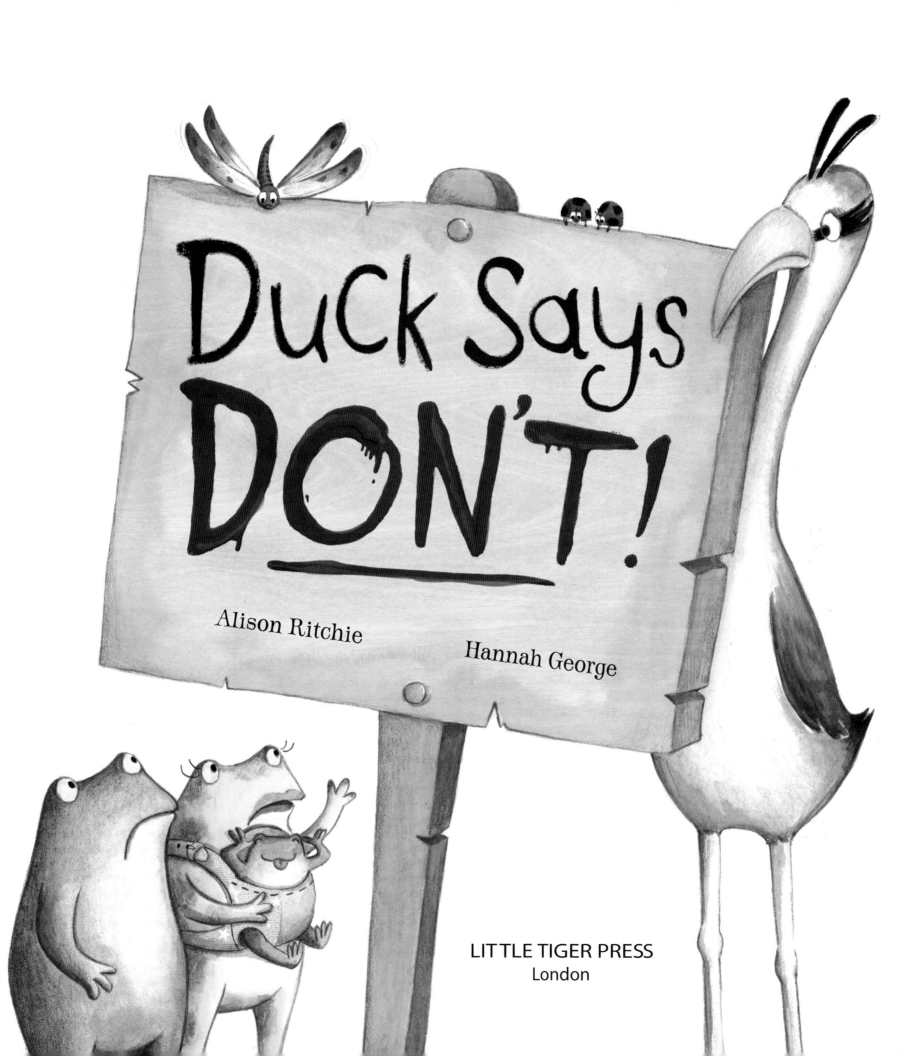

Duck Says DON'T!

Alison Ritchie

Hannah George

LITTLE TIGER PRESS
London

Duck lived on Goose's pond.
It was a **beautiful** pond. The water
was clear and sparkly, the sun shone
and everyone was **happy**.

One day, Goose told Duck, "I have a **very** important job for you. I am going on holiday, and I want **you** to look after the pond while I'm away."

Duck could **not** believe it.

"Goose wants me to look after the pond," he thought. "I am in charge!"

"Goose, I will do my very best," he promised.

The next day, Duck was up early watching over his beautiful pond. Suddenly he spotted the dragonflies racing.

"Stop that!" he quacked. "I am in charge of this pond, and you should **not** be buzzing about all over it!"

FINISH LINE

"We're flying, Duck," said the dragonflies in surprise. "That's what we do!"
   "Not here you don't," said Duck.

"That's told them," he thought. But just to make sure, Duck fetched some wood, and hammered late into the night…

The next morning there was a sign in the pond.

Later that day, Duck saw Kingfisher fishing.

"Hey!" he shouted. "Stop that!

Fishing is not allowed here."

"Then where can I fish?"
said Kingfisher sadly.
"Somewhere else!" snapped Duck,
and he waddled off with his bottom in the air.

He fetched more wood and got busy
with another sign.

Duck was just having a little nap when
the frogs dived into the water,

SPLASH!

"Frogs!" Duck yelled.
"What do you think you're doing?
Diving is forbidden!"

"Forbidden?"
said the frogs angrily. "Says who?"
"Says me," snapped Duck. "Duck!
Duck in charge of the pond!
So get out right now!"

Soon there were signs up **everywhere!**

NO DIVING
Diving is STRICTLY
Forbidden
(because Duck says so!)

NO RU...

NO SPLASHING

NO SU...

Duck sat down happily. "Peace at last!" he thought.
But he couldn't settle. He looked at his perfect pond.
The sun was shining, the air was still
and there was
not a splash, buzz or
plop to be heard.

NO DIVING
Diving is STRICTLY
Forbidden
(because Duck says So!)

NO RUNNING!

NO SPLASHING

NO JUMPING

NO SWIMMING

POND LIFE

In fact there was
nothing
to be heard. It was
much
too
quiet!

RACING!
der of Duck
(in charge of pond)

O FISHING
UCK'S RULE (must be obeyed)

"Where is everyone?"
wailed Duck. "What have I done?"
He jumped up in a panic and
flew off to find his friends.

As Duck reached the meadow, he saw them playing together.

"This is fun," buzzed the dragonflies. "No bossy Duck telling us off!" croaked the frogs.

A tear fell down Duck's cheek. With a heavy heart he turned around and waddled back to Goose's pond.

The friends were snoozing in the afternoon sun
when they heard hammering coming from the pond.
"Can you believe it?" muttered the frogs.
"That duck is putting up **more** signs!"

The banging went on deep into the night.
Next morning there was an **enormous**
sign in the meadow…

Duck is Very, Very SORRY!

PLEASE COME BACK.

This message is for the dragonflies, frogs and kingfisher, from Duck xx

When the friends arrived at Goose's pond, they saw other signs too:

RACING welcome

FREE fishing rods

NEW diving board

RUNNING,
JUMPING,
SWIMMING and
SPLASHING
Allowed!

"Silly Duck!"
chirped Kingfisher.
"We've missed you!"
"Even though you were **very** bossy,"
chuckled the frogs.

When Goose came back from holiday,
she said, "Duck, you've done a **grand job**!
I'll leave you in charge next time."

"No thank you, Goose." Duck laughed. "Being in charge is much too hard!"

And from that day on, Goose's pond was the **happiest** pond in the world, and Duck never said another bossy word.

Duck says: "Don't miss these great Little Tiger books!"

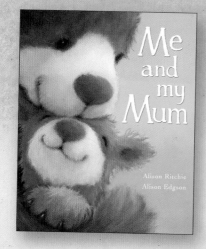

Me and my Mum

Alison Ritchie
Alison Edgson

Super-Duper Dudley!

Sue Mongredien

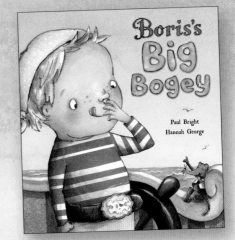

Boris's Big Bogey

Paul Bright
Hannah George

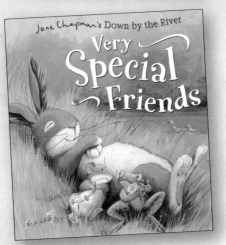

Jane Chapman's Down by the River

Very Special Friends

A NEW Lazy Ladybird Adventure

Look Out, Ladybird!

Jack Tickle

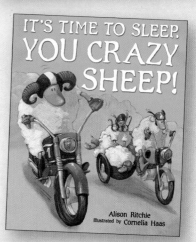

IT'S TIME TO SLEEP, YOU CRAZY SHEEP!

Alison Ritchie
Illustrated by Cornelia Haas

For information regarding any of the above titles or for our catalogue, please contact us:
Little Tiger Press, 1 The Coda Centre,
189 Munster Road, London SW6 6AW
Tel: 020 7385 6333 • Fax: 020 7385 7333
E-mail: info@littletiger.co.uk • www.littletigerpress.com